The Golden
CIRCUS

By Kathryn JACKSON
Illustrated by
Alice and Martin PROVENSEN

A GOLDEN BOOK • NEW YORK

Library of Congress Control Number: 2004103554
ISBN: 0-375-83215-7 (trade)—ISBN: 0-375-93215-1 (lib. bdg.)
www.goldenbooks.com
MANUFACTURED IN CHINA   First Random House Edition 2005
10 9 8 7 6 5 4 3 2 1

MR. ROLY-POLY was a jolly man who loved the circus so much that he made up his mind to have one of his very own.

"I'll call it Roly-Poly's Circus," he promised himself. "And it will be the biggest, brightest, jolliest, most exciting circus in the whole world!"

He went straight out and got himself a brave
lion tamer who could snap his whip CRACK!
CRACK! CRACK!—louder and faster than any
other lion tamer anywhere—

—and a great, fierce lion that lashed its tail, opened
its jaws and roared: "Hr-r-r-r-ahhhh!"
It was the loudest, fiercest lion roar that ever was.

Mr. Roly-Poly bought seals that balanced balls on their pointed noses, and turned back somersaults, and clapped their flippers CLAP! CLAP! CLAP!—much faster than any other seals in the whole world.

He chose a skating bear that whizzed round and round
on silver skates. Faster and faster it went, nose in the air,
paws out in front, and it never once fell down.

"That's the bear for me!" said Mr. Roly-Poly.

He found a fat lady so fat you could hardly believe your eyes—

A thin man so thin you had to look twice to see him—

And the biggest, gayest, most magnificent elephants ever, each one bigger, gayer, and more magnificent than the rest—

And a man-on-the-flying-trapeze who swung from such dizzying, dazzling heights that it was hard to know whether to hold your breath or scream!

The giraffe Mr. Roly-Poly bought was so tall that the new circus man had to lean way back to see its head.

"It's the tallest giraffe in captivity!" he said proudly.

Then he went looking for lots and lots of
clowns; the drollest, funniest, most absurd
and ridiculous clowns in the whole world.

He got the kind that take off dozens of
coats, and the kind that go to a fire, the kind

that stare at you until you don't know where to look, the extremely tall kind, the short fat kind, and even the kind that is a little dog dressed as a clown.

"Now for horses!" Mr. Roly-Poly cried.

He took only the sleekest and most beautiful of dancing horses, and only the most daring and beautiful ladies to dance and balance on their backs.

"Nothing but the best for Roly-Poly's Circus," said Mr. Roly-Poly, buying more and more wonderful things.

At last his circus was all ready to try out!

Mr. Roly-Poly sat in his enormous, brand-new circus tent and watched the show from beginning to end.

But somehow it wasn't the biggest, brightest, jolliest, most exciting circus at all. Nothing seemed right. Even the clowns seemed poky and dull.

"Something is wrong with my circus!" Mr. Roly-Poly
said. "Something is missing!"

But what could it be?

The new circus man thought and thought and thought,
but he could not think what was missing.

He asked the lion tamer, but he didn't know.

He asked the lion

and the big kangaroo

and the little kangaroo—

But they didn't know what was missing.

But they sadly agreed that SOMETHING was wrong.

"Well," said Mr. Roly-Poly, "now I just don't know what can be missing. Now I just give up!"

He almost began to cry.

Almost, but not quite—

—because at that very moment, his biggest, gayest, and most magnificent elephant leaned its trunk on his shoulder.

"Know what this circus needs?" it asked.

And it whispered softly in Mr. Roly-Poly's ear.

The seals were close enough to hear that whisper.

"That's right!" they barked. "That's exactly what we need. And if we had THAT, we'd clap most merrily, like this—"

They clapped so happily that Mr. Roly-Poly began to feel jolly again.

Away he ran, waving his arms and calling back:

"I'll go and get what's missing!"

THE GREATEST PERFORMANCE
in the History of
THE GREATEST SHOW ON EARTH

When the skating bear heard that, it put on its skates and jumped over six barrels in a row.

The leader of the horses kicked much higher than ever before.

And the tumblers and acrobats and strong men ran out into the big center ring and began to do all their tricks at the very same time.

What a splendid sight that was!

It made the lion feel so happy that it just had to roar.
Roar it did.
And what a roar!
"HUR-R-R-R-R-AHHHHHH!"
It was a roar to make your hair stand on end!

The clowns pretended to be frightened.

They climbed up each other, up and up, higher and higher, looking so funny that everyone in the circus began to laugh.

Then everyone began to cheer, too, because they heard the most wonderful, loud, jolly circus music coming closer and closer, and closer—

—and into the tent marched Mr. Roly-Poly, with a brand-new, exciting, jolly circus band! The drums boomed, the cymbals clanged, the shining horns tooted.

"There!" called Mr. Roly-Poly. "There's our band! Now there's nothing missing! NOW let's see what kind of show we can put on!"

And this time, when he watched his circus, the band played from beginning to end. It played such splendid, stirring music that every act was twice as funny and exciting as ever before, and three times as big and bright and jolly and exciting as any other circus anywhere, any time, in all the whole world!

"I owe it all to you," said Mr. Roly-Poly to his biggest, gayest, most magnificent elephant.

"It was nothing at all." The elephant smiled.

But just the same, Mr. Roly-Poly insisted that the elephant lead the circus parade ever after, and there's NOTHING an elephant likes better than that!